Hello, you!

Oh, please don't **look** inside the pages of this **book**.

Turn around and quickly **run** ...

The
SCHOOL
of
MONSTERS
has **begun!**

THIS BOOK
BELONGS TO

SCHOOL OF MONSTERS

By Sally Rippin

JEM'S BIG IDEA

Art by Chris Kennett

Kane Miller
A DIVISION OF EDC PUBLISHING

This is Jem.
She's very fast.

When monsters race, she's never **last**.

Up and down,

inside and **out**.

"Go, Jem, go!"
the others **shout**.

When monsters need
to climb the **stairs**,

they often walk
with Jem in **pairs.**

Sometimes two and sometimes **more**,

they carry Jem right
to the **door**.

One day when they all play **outside**,

it soon becomes Jem's turn to **hide**.

Jem is fast and Jem is **strong**.

But Jem is never hidden **long**.

Jem tries to look for somewhere **new** –

wheels are fast,
but tricky too.

"We found you, Jem!"
the others **say**.

Jem wants to find another **way**.

So Jem invents
a special **plan.**

Can she do it?

Yes, she can!

SPROING!

The next day when the monsters **play,**

they close their eyes
and hear Jem **say** ...

"This time there's nowhere I can't **go**.

BAA -

Come and find me.
Don't be **slow!**"

DOING!

They count to ten and
then they **yell**.

But Jem is hidden
far too **well**.

They search the school,
they search the **yard**.

The monsters roar
and laugh with glee

when they see Jem
up in the tree.

Jem is fast, but clever, too –

there's really nothing
Jem can't **do**!

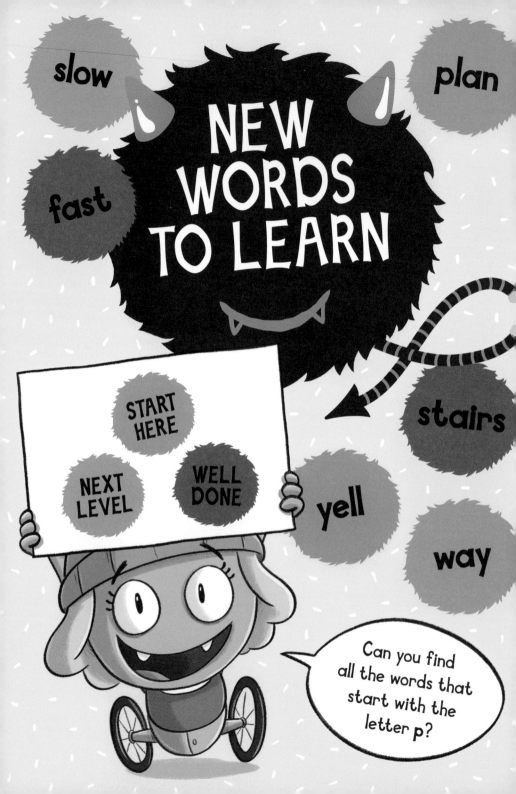

HOW TO USE THIS BOOK

for adults reading with children

Welcome to the School of Monsters!

Here are some tips for helping your child learn to read.

At first, your child will be happy just to listen to you read aloud. Reading to your child is a great way for them to associate books with enjoyment and love, as well as to become familiar with language. Talk to them about what is going on in the pictures and ask them questions about what they see. As you read aloud, follow the words with your finger from left to right.

Once your child has started to receive some basic reading instruction, you might like to point out the words in **bold**. Some of these will already be familiar from school. You can assist your child to decode the ones they don't know by sounding out the letters.

As your child's confidence increases, you might like to pause at each word in bold and let your child try to sound it out for themselves. They can then practice the words again using the list at the back of the book.

After some time, your child may feel ready to tackle the whole story themselves. Maybe they can make up their own monster stories, too!

Sally Rippin is one of Australia's best-selling and most-beloved children's authors. She has written over 50 books for children and young adults, and her mantel holds numerous awards for her writing. Best known for her *Billie B. Brown, Hey Jack!* and *Polly and Buster* series, Sally loves to write stories with heart, as well as characters that resonate with children, parents, and teachers alike.

HOW TO DRAW JEM

① Using a pencil, start with 2 circles for eyes and a wide, happy mouth. Underneath the face, draw a big U shape for her chin.

② Above the face draw a bendy rectangle and a semicircle for a hat. Add 2 horns and 2 pointy teeth.

③ Add some tufts of hair behind her head and a round circle for her belly.

④ Divide the belly in half. Now draw some tubes for arms and wheel supports.

5. Draw in her hands and 2 ovals for wheels. Use an eraser to remove the overlapping lines, if you have one.

6. Time for the final details! Draw in some eyelashes and add details to her body. Don't forget the spokes on her awesome wheels!

Chris Kennett has been drawing ever since he could hold a pencil (or so his mom says). But professionally, Chris has been creating quirky characters for just over 20 years. He's best known for drawing weird and wonderful creatures from the *Star Wars* universe, but he also loves drawing cute and cuddly monsters – and he hopes you do too!

WELCOME
TO THE

SCHOOL OF MONSTERS

You shouldn't bring a pet to **school**. But Mary's pet is super **cool!**

SCHOOL OF MONSTERS
By Sally Rippin
MARY HAS THE BEST PET
Art by Chris Kennett

Have you read **ALL** the School of Monsters stories?

Sam makes a mess when he eats **jam**. Can he fix it? Yes, he **can!**

SCHOOL OF MONSTERS
By Sally Rippin
HAIRY SAM LOVES BREAD AND JAM
Art by Chris Kennett

SCHOOL OF MONSTERS
By Sally Rippin
PETE'S BIG FEET
Art by Chris Kennett

Today it's Sports Day in the **sun**. But do you think that Pete can **run?**

SCHOOL OF MONSTERS
By Sally Rippin
JAMIE LEE'S BIRTHDAY TREAT
Art by Chris Kennett

Jamie Lee sure likes to **eat!** Today she has a special **treat** ...

When Bat-Boy Tim comes out to **play**, why do others run **away**?

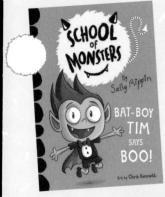

No one likes to be left **out**.
This makes Luna scream and **shout**!

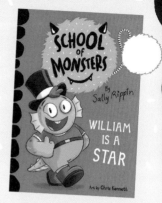

When Will gets nervous, he lets out a **stink**.
But what will all his classmates **think**?

Some monsters are short, and others are **tall**, but Frank is quite clearly the tallest of **all**!

All that Jess touches gets gooey and **sticky**.
How can she solve a problem so **tricky**?

When Bug starts school he cannot **read**.
But Teacher has the help he **needs**!

This is Jem. She likes to **play**, and thinks up fun new ways each **day**!

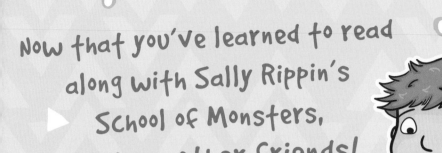

Now that you've learned to read along with Sally Rippin's School of Monsters, meet her other friends!

Hey Jack!

Billie B. Brown

Down-to-earth, real-life stories for real-life kids!

Billie B. Brown is brave, brilliant and bold, and she always has a creative way to save the day!

Jack has a big heart and an even bigger imagination. He's Billie's best friend, and he'd love to be your friend, too!

Jem's Big Idea

First American Edition 2023
Kane Miller, A Division of EDC Publishing

Text copyright © 2022 Sally Rippin
Illustration copyright © 2022 Chris Kennett
Series design copyright © 2022 Hardie Grant Children's Publishing
First published in 2022 by Hardie Grant Children's Publishing
Ground Floor, Building 1, 658 Church Street Richmond,
Victoria 3121, Australia.

For information contact:
Kane Miller, A Division of EDC Publishing
5402 S 122nd E Ave, Tulsa, OK 74146
www.kanemiller.com

Library of Congress Control Number: 2022941816

ISBN: 978-1-68464-636-4

Printed in China
by Leo Paper Group
10 9 8 7 6 5 4 3 2 1